# Here Comes
# Firefighter Hippo

## Jonathan London
### ILLUSTRATED BY Gilles Eduar

BOYDS MILLS PRESS
AN IMPRINT OF HIGHLIGHTS
*Honesdale, Pennsylvania*

For Sean & Steph, Aaron, and sweet Maureen
—JL

For information about permissions to reproduce selections from
this book, please contact permissions@highlights.com.

Boyds Mills Press, Inc.
815 Church Street
Honesdale, Pennsylvania 18431
boydsmillspress.com
Printed in Atlanta, GA

ISBN: 978-1-59078-968-1

Library of Congress Control Number: 2013931089

First edition
The text is set in Baileywick Gothic.
The illustrations are done in gouache.
10 9 8 7 6 5 4 3 2 1

**Little Hippo** didn't like being little. In fact, he liked to dress up and pretend that he was big. So one day, he jumped into his fire truck and pedaled off—*zoom!*—to play firefighter—*ding-a-ling! ding-a-ling!*

He rushed by Big Hippo, who was wallowing in a mud hole, and—thunk! Firefighter Hippo got stuck in the muck.

"Help!" cried the little fireman. "I am Firefighter Hippo, and I have to fight a fire!" So . . .

Big Hippo bumped and thumped and—plup!—pushed the fire truck out.

**"Thanks!"** said Firefighter Hippo, and he zoomed off—
*ding-a-ling! ding-a-ling!*

Then he sped by Graceful Gazelle,
who was grazing on small shrubs, and—uuurch!
Firefighter Hippo got caught in the tall grass.

"Help!" cried the little fireman.
"I am Firefighter Hippo, and I have to fight a fire!" So . . .

Graceful Gazelle used his horns and—Snik!—pulled the fire truck out.

**"Thanks!"** said Firefighter Hippo, and he zoomed off— *ding-a-ling! ding-a-ling!*

Now Firefighter Hippo chugged up a steep hill,
where Very Tall Giraffe was nibbling leaves.
Chug, chug, chug—"UGH!"
Little Hippo could not climb any higher.

"Help!" cried the little fireman. "I am Firefighter Hippo,
and I have to fight a fire!" So . . .

Very Tall Giraffe lifted Firefighter Hippo—
and his fire truck—up . . .

up . . .

up . . .

then lowered him

down . . .

down . . .

down . . .

to the top of the hill.

"Thanks!" said Firefighter Hippo,
and he zoomed off—
*ding-a-ling! ding-a-ling!*

Then he passed by Laughing Hyena and said, "Hello! I am Firefighter Hippo, and I have to fight a fire!"

*"Hee-hee! Ha-ha! Ho-ho!"* laughed Hyena. "You're a VERY little firefighter!"

"NO I'M NOT!" said Firefighter Hippo. So . . .

. . . he sat TALL and raced by Lion and said, "Hello! I am Firefighter Hippo, and I have to fight a fire!"

But Lion was asleep, and he made a very loud and scary SNOOOAAAAARRRRRRRRR! So . . .

Firefighter Hippo raced even faster. Just then he saw a flash of lightning and heard the Ka-BOOOOOOOM! of thunder, and off in the distance Firefighter Hippo saw a small tree burst into flame! Ka-RRRAAAAACK!

**"FIRE! FIRE!"** he yelled, and he zoomed off to look for help— *ding-a-ling! ding-a-ling!*

Nearby, he found Elephant, who was drinking at a water hole. "Help!" cried the little fireman. "I am Firefighter Hippo—and there's a FIRE!"

Elephant ran to the tree, and Firefighter Hippo climbed his fire ladder, up . . . up . . . up . . .

and held on to Elephant's trunk—SPLOOOOOOOOOOOSH!—
and helped put the fire OUT!

"Hip-hippo-ray!" trumpeted Elephant. "You saved the day!"
"Thanks!" said Firefighter Hippo, and he climbed down . . . down . . . down.

Then he jumped in his fire truck and zoomed all the way home—
*ding-a-ling! ding-a-ling!*

"Where have you been, Little Hippo?" asked Mama Hippo.
"I've been fighting a fire!" he said, beaming a big smile. "I saw Big Hippo,
Graceful Gazelle, Very Tall Giraffe, Laughing Hyena, Lion, and Elephant!
And with a little help from Elephant, I PUT THE FIRE *OUT*!"

"Oh, you're a *brave* little fireman!" said Mama Hippo.
"Now," said Little Hippo, "I'll show you how a firefighter
waters the garden!" And he squirted his fire hose . . .

SQUIRT! SQUIRT! "Oops!" said the little fireman, and he giggled—
*Ha-ha! Ho-ho!* Mama laughed and squirted Little Hippo back with her garden hose.

And they had the greatest mud fight in the history of the jungle!
SPLISH! SPLOP! *SPLAT!*